JAMES to the
RESCUE

The Masterpiece Adventures BOOK TWO

JAMES to the RESCUE

ELISE BROACH

Illustrated by
KELLY MURPHY

SQUARE FISH

Christy Ottaviano Books

Henry Holt and Company • NEW YORK

SQUARE FISH

An imprint of Macmillan Publishing Group, LLC
175 Fifth Avenue
New York, NY 10010
mackids.com

Square Fish and the Square Fish logo are trademarks of Macmillan and
are used by Henry Holt and Company under license from Macmillan.

Our books may be purchased in bulk for promotional, educational, or business use. Please
contact your local bookseller or the Macmillan Corporate and Premium Sales Department at
(800) 221-7945 ext. 5442 or by e-mail at MacmillanSpecialMarkets@macmillan.com.

Library of Congress Cataloging-in-Publication Data

Broach, Elise.
James to the rescue / Elise Broach ; illustrated by Kelly Murphy.
pages   cm. — (The masterpiece adventures ; book 2)
"Christy Ottaviano Books."
Summary: "Marvin the beetle is going collecting with his family. All is well and good
until Uncle Albert gets hurt. Marvin needs his human friend James's help
to save Uncle Albert before it's too late"— Provided by publisher.
ISBN 978-1-250-10378-9 (paperback) — ISBN 978-1-62779-317-9 (e-book) [1. Beetles—Fiction.
2. Human-animal relationships—Fiction. 3. Friendship—Fiction. 4. Collectors and collecting—
Fiction. 5. Rescues—Fiction.] I. Murphy, Kelly, 1977– illustrator. II. Title.
PZ7.B78083Jam 2015   [Fic]—dc23   2014042196

Originally published in the United States by Christy
Ottaviano Books/Henry Holt and Company
First Square Fish Edition: 2017
Book designed by April Ward and Anna Booth
Square Fish logo designed by Filomena Tuosto
The artist used pen and ink on Coventry Rag paper to
create the illustrations for this book.

1   3   5   7   9   10   8   6   4   2

AR: 3.0 / LEXILE: 480L

For Christy Ottaviano, whose wondrous editing
has rescued me again and again

—E. B.

For Gretchen, a friend always to the rescue

—K. M.

Contents

CHAPTER ONE
Collecting

Marvin is excited. Papa and Uncle Albert are going collecting. Collecting is what the beetles call it when they crawl around the Pompadays' apartment looking for things they can use.

A button can make a pretty table.

A doll's shoe can be a nice chair.

A cap from a tube of toothpaste can hold a giant feast.

For the first time ever, Marvin and Elaine get to go collecting. There's no telling what they will find. They are so excited that they do a happy dance, like this:

Mama is not so excited.

"Please be careful," she says. "Collecting is dangerous! You must listen to Papa and Uncle Albert."

"We will," Marvin promises.

"We're going to have the BEST time!" Elaine says. "I know we'll find something really good."

"I hope so," Marvin says.

Marvin thinks about what he would like to find.

He might find part of a crayon . . .

Or a tiny piece of wrapping paper . . .

Or something to put inside his secret
hideout.

"Ready?" Papa says.

"YES!" Marvin and Elaine shout.

Papa and Uncle Albert have a little
sack that they drag by the string. It's
blue and silky. It used to hold a pair of
Mrs. Pompaday's earrings. Now it's the
perfect bag for collecting.

"Let's go," says Uncle Albert.

Papa, Uncle Albert, Marvin, and Elaine sneak out of their home in the kitchen cupboard.

William, James's baby brother, is in the kitchen. He's banging a spoon on the floor.

Bang! Bang! Bang!

The beetles do not like William. They hide near the leg of a chair.

But William sees them.

"Ba ba!" William says.

Uh-oh! He crawls across the floor, banging his spoon.

BANG! BANG! BANG!

The beetles race away from him.

William crawls after them.

"BA BA!" he yells.

William raises his spoon over their heads.

"Stop, drop, and roll!" Papa cries.

The beetles all roll into little balls.

But then they hear Mrs. Pompaday.

"Shhhh, William," she says. "It's time for your nap."

William starts to cry. She picks him up and carries him away, her high heels clicking on the floor.

Click, click, click.

"Phew!" says Uncle Albert. "That was a close one. Let's go to James's room."

"Wait," Elaine says. "I found something."

Marvin sees crumbs under the table, but those are nothing special. The beetles find crumbs all the time.

But then he sees something else,
something that Elaine is already racing
toward at full speed.

Something shiny.

Something silver.

CHAPTER TWO

Something Good

It's a dime!

Elaine is so excited she runs in circles.

"Well done, Elaine!" Uncle Albert
says. "That will make a fine silver platter
for your mother."

"I know!" Elaine says. "She'll love it."

Elaine looks smug. Marvin feels bad. He wants to find a present for Mama, but there is nothing else in the kitchen.

"A dime is heavy," Papa says. He and Uncle Albert huff and puff as they roll it into the blue sack. Then they drag the sack behind them, still huffing and puffing.

"Let's go to James's room now," Papa
says. "We always have good luck there."

The beetles crawl down the hallway
to James's bedroom.

"My dime is beautiful," Elaine tells
Marvin. "I knew I would find something
really good."

Marvin is quiet. He wants Elaine to stop talking about the dime.

But she doesn't stop.

"I bet I'll get to go collecting again," Elaine says, "because I found something special."

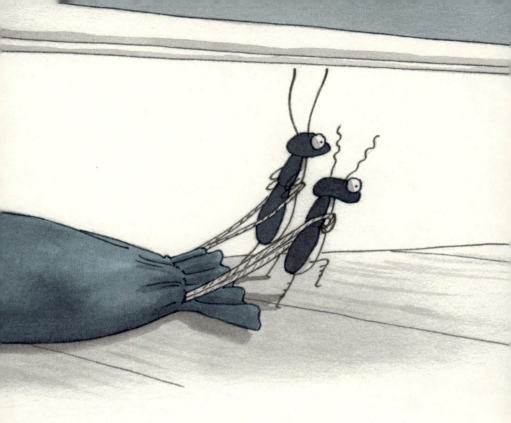

When Marvin doesn't answer, she asks, "Don't you wish YOU had found that dime?"

Now Elaine is really pushing it. Marvin glares at her.

"I'm going to find something even better," he tells her.

"Well," Elaine says, "I can't think of anything better than a dime."

Marvin rushes ahead, through the door of James's room. He wants so badly to find something really good.

James is lying on his bed reading.
Marvin is always happy to see James.
He wishes he could climb up on James's
desk to say hello, but he knows Papa
and Uncle Albert don't want James to
notice them.

The beetles crawl over the carpet to the wastebasket. When James throws things away, sometimes they fall on the carpet.

Papa finds a bright orange tack from James's bulletin board. He puts it in the sack.

Uncle Albert finds an old piece of gum. It's still a bit sticky.

"Perfect," he says. "We can use this to hang pictures in the living room."

Marvin hasn't found anything.

He sighs. Maybe he's not good at collecting. Maybe Papa and Uncle Albert will only take Elaine next time.

But then, just as he is about to give up, he sees something.

It's small and black and has a pointy tip. He runs over to it as fast as he can, before Elaine can grab it.

"Look!" he says, lifting it with two of his legs. It's heavy.

"What is that thing?" Elaine asks.

Papa and Uncle Albert come over to take a look.

"Hmmm," Papa says. "I have no idea. What do you think, Albert?"

Uncle Albert shakes his head. "It's smooth," he says, touching it. "And it has a sharp tip. But I've never seen anything like it before."

"Huh," Elaine says. "I don't know what anyone would use that for."

"It's interesting," Marvin says.

It *is* interesting—shiny and black
and smooth, with a sharp point.

"Put it in the sack," Papa says.

"But what's it good for?" Elaine
wants to know.

Marvin is mad at Elaine. "It's good for something," he says, putting the sharp black thing in the blue sack. "And it's different from a regular old dime."

"Okay, you two," Uncle Albert says. "That's enough. Let's look in the bathroom."

Marvin wishes they didn't have to leave James without saying hello, or good-bye. But Papa and Uncle Albert are busy collecting. They lead the way down the hall to the bathroom.

"I can't wait to give my mother that dime," Elaine says to Marvin. "She'll be so happy."

Marvin tries to ignore her.

"Too bad you haven't found anything good yet," Elaine says.

"I did find something good," Marvin says. But he doesn't really believe it. If he gives the pointy black thing to Mama, what will she do with it?

At last they reach the bathroom.
They crawl across the cold, slippery
tiles. The tiles by the toilet are wet,
because the pipe behind
the toilet leaks.

Marvin slips and slides.

"Yuck," Elaine says, wiping her legs
on her shell.

They are just starting to look around
the bottom of the sink when Uncle
Albert shouts with joy.

"Eureka!"

"What?" Elaine asks. "What is it?"

"He's found something," Papa says excitedly. Uncle Albert races over to a tiny pair of scissors that are lying on the floor behind the toilet. They're made of metal and very shiny. They are the smallest scissors Marvin has ever seen.

"Nail scissors!" Papa cries. "What a find. Good work, Albert."

Marvin remembers Mama saying how wonderful it would be to have something she could use for cutting. The beetles can chew through soft

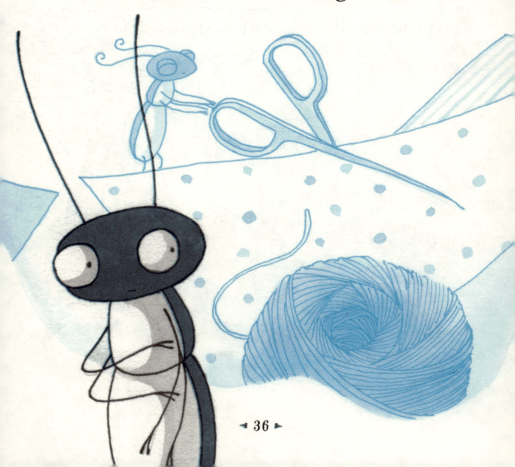

stuff, but they can't cut in a straight line. Only scissors can do that. Scissors can cut paper, or string, or a piece of cloth. They can cut things into small pieces, with no messy edges.

Marvin wishes so badly that he had seen the scissors first.

"Look at these beauties!" Uncle Albert says. "I can't wait to show them to Edith."

He tries to put them in the sack, but they won't fit.

"Hmmm," he says. "They're too big. Marvin, you and Elaine will have to pull the sack. Your father and I will carry the scissors."

But just as Uncle Albert is bending over to lift the pointed end of the scissors, his back legs slip on the wet floor.

Whoosh!

He falls against the sharp point of the scissors.

"Ooomph! OHHHHHH!" he cries.

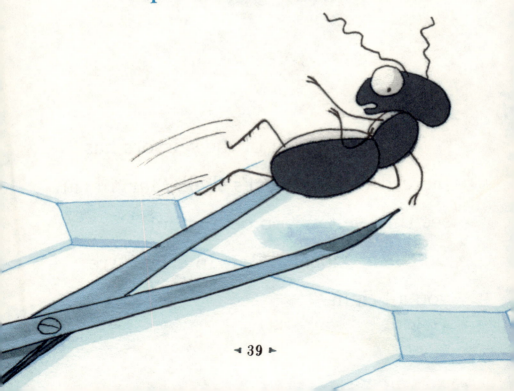

CHAPTER THREE

Uncle Albert in Trouble

Oh no!

The sharp point of the scissors has pierced Uncle Albert's shell. Marvin can see thin yellow goo oozing out.

"Uncle Albert!" Marvin cries. "Are you all right?"

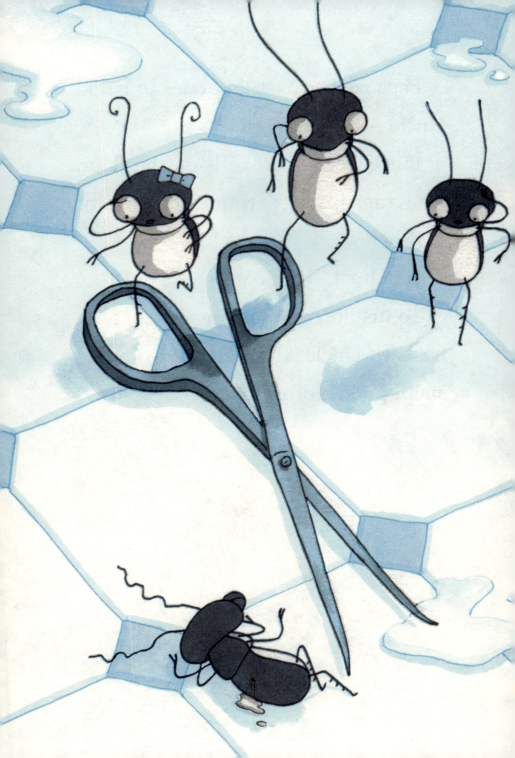

Papa rushes over and tries to help Uncle Albert stand up.

But Uncle Albert rolls on the floor. He wraps his legs around the hole in his shell.

"I'm hurt," he moans.

To his horror, Marvin sees that beneath Uncle Albert, there is now a small puddle of yellow goo.

"Oh, my poor father!" Elaine screams.

"Marvin! Elaine! Quick, get a tissue," Papa says. "We need to stop the bleeding."

There's a tissue box on top of the toilet. Marvin and Elaine run up the side of the toilet as fast as they can.

There is a tissue sticking out of the box. They each grab a corner of it. They pull and pull.

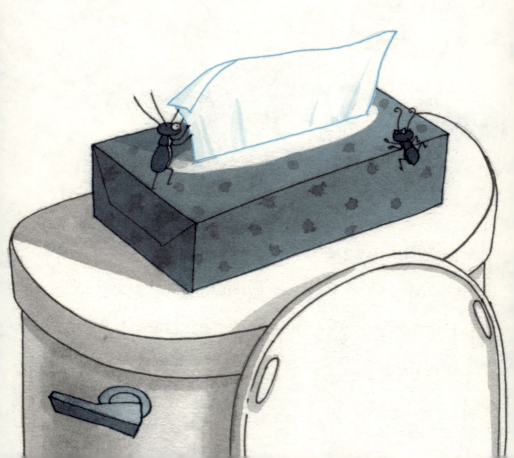

"Hurry!" Papa calls.

"Quick, Elaine," Marvin says. "Pull as hard as you can."

They pull on the corners of the tissue. They pull harder.

Suddenly, it comes flying out of the box!

"Hold on tight!" Marvin tells Elaine.

"I am!" Elaine cries.

Gripping the corners, Marvin and
Elaine sail through the air. The tissue
billows over them, like a parachute.

Far below is the bathroom floor, where Papa and Uncle Albert are waiting.

Marvin and Elaine flutter down, down, down until they reach the floor. It's like they are jumping out of a plane. A rescue plane.

"Nice work," Papa says.

He tears a strip of tissue and gently wraps it around Uncle Albert's shell. "This will stop the bleeding," he says.

"Oooooohhhh," Uncle Albert moans. His eyes roll back in his head.

"Okay," Papa says grimly. "Let's try to move him."

Papa picks up Uncle Albert's head.

Marvin and Elaine pick up his two back legs.

They try to lift him.

"**OOOOOOHHHHHHH!**" Uncle Albert screams.

"Stop! Stop!" Elaine cries. "We're hurting him. Oh, my dear father . . . what are we to do?"

"I can't move," Uncle Albert says. "You'll have to go back without me."

"No, Albert, we won't leave you," Papa says. "There must be a way to get you home."

"Oh, there must be!" Elaine cries.

"But how?"

They all gather around Uncle Albert.

What are they going to do?

Then Marvin has an idea.

"I'll get James!" he says.

"Do you think that's safe?" Papa asks.

Papa and Mama know all about Marvin's friendship with James. They know that Marvin trusts James more than anyone in the world. But because James is a boy, and Marvin is a beetle, they still worry.

"Yes, Papa," Marvin says. "James will help us."

Papa looks at Uncle Albert. He looks at Marvin. "Then go, son," he says. "There isn't much time."

CHAPTER FOUR
James to the Rescue!

As fast as he can, Marvin runs across the tile floor and down the hallway, to James's bedroom.

He crawls across the blue shag rug. James is still lying on his bed reading.

Marvin crawls up the bedpost and over the open pages of the book.

Of course, James sees him.

"Hey, little guy," he says, smiling. "Where have you been?"

Marvin is desperate. He runs around in a circle.

"What's the matter?" James asks, sitting up.

Marvin flips onto his back and waves his legs in the air.

"Something's wrong," James says. "Are you hurt?" He reaches down with one finger and rolls Marvin back onto his legs.

Marvin scrambles onto James's finger and runs to the very tip. This is how he tells James where to go.

James stands up. "Okay, where to?" he asks, holding out his finger, with Marvin on the tip.

James walks out of his room, carrying Marvin on his finger. But then, uh-oh, James turns right toward the kitchen, instead of left toward the bathroom—the wrong way! Marvin crawls down James's finger, to the palm of his hand. This is how he tells James he is going the wrong way.

"The other way?" James asks. He turns
and starts down the hall toward the
bathroom. Marvin races back to the tip
of his finger.

Now they are at the bathroom door.

There, on the floor by the toilet, are
Papa, Elaine, and Uncle Albert.

As soon as Papa and Elaine see James,
they run behind the toilet. But Uncle
Albert is badly hurt. He lies on his side,
not moving.

James looks around the room. "Why do you want to come in here?"

Marvin begins to jump up and down on James's finger.

"Do you want me to put you down?" James asks. "Okay, little guy. Show me what you want me to see."

Gently, he sets his finger on the floor
so that Marvin can crawl off. Marvin
runs to where Uncle Albert is lying.
Marvin can see that more yellow goo
has oozed onto the tissue that Papa
used to bandage Uncle Albert's shell.

"Oh!" James says. "Who's this? One of your friends?"

Slowly, James bends down.

"What's wrong with him?" James asks Marvin. "Is he dead?"

Behind the toilet, Elaine gasps. Uncle Albert waves his legs weakly.

"No, look, he's moving," James says. "What happened to him?"

Marvin crawls over to the tiny silver scissors and taps the sharp point with his front legs.

"Oh!" James says. "He's hurt! He cut himself on the nail scissors. I've done that before. They're sharp."

Uncle Albert moans again, and closes his eyes.

Marvin stands next to him, full of despair. He looks up at James and wonders how in the world James can help them.

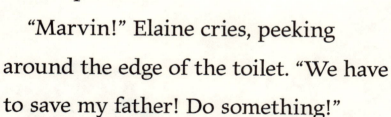

"Marvin!" Elaine cries, peeking around the edge of the toilet. "We have to save my father! Do something!"

James is already kneeling on the floor, leaning over Uncle Albert.

Gently, he picks him up. Uncle Albert groans, but this time, James says to Marvin, "Don't worry. I have an idea."

And just like that, Marvin stops worrying. He knows that James will be able to help.

James holds Uncle Albert in his hand.

He peels off the old tissue. He takes a new tissue and puts it in the sink. He turns on the faucet just a little.

Drip, drop, drip.

With the new, wet tissue, he dabs the
hole in Uncle Albert's shell.

"Owwwww! Owwwww!" Uncle
Albert cries.

"Marvin! James is killing him!"
Elaine shouts.

"No, Elaine, it's okay," Marvin tells
her. "James knows what to do."

James opens the medicine cabinet over the sink. He takes out a small green-and-white tube.

"This is what we put on cuts," he tells Marvin, "so they don't get infected."

Marvin doesn't know what *infected* means, but it sounds bad. James takes the cap off the tube and squeezes it. A tiny, clear blob comes out.

Carefully, with the tip of his finger, James pats the blob over the hole in Uncle Albert's shell. The yellow goo stops oozing out.

"There," James says. "That's better."

Marvin can see that it *is* better. He's filled with relief.

James takes a new, clean tissue and puts Uncle Albert inside it.

Then he holds out his finger so
Marvin can climb back up.

"Where do you want me to take
him?" James asks Marvin. "Back to the
cupboard?"

Marvin smiles. Of course James
would know what to do! He always
understands. Marvin runs to the tip
of James's finger.

James lifts the tissue carrying Uncle Albert.

Marvin holds on tight. Far below, he can see Papa and Elaine watching from behind the toilet. He waves to them so that they'll know everything is all right.

When they get to the kitchen, James
bends down next to the cupboard
where the beetles live and opens the
door. Gently, he puts Uncle Albert's
tissue inside the cupboard. Marvin
crawls off his finger.

"I hope your friend will be okay," he tells Marvin. Marvin looks up at James, his heart full of thanks.

Then James quickly closes the cupboard door, before Mr. or Mrs. Pompaday can notice him.

As soon as the cupboard is dark and safe, Marvin calls, "Mama! Aunt Edith! Uncle Albert is hurt!"

Then he holds one of Uncle Albert's legs and waits for help to arrive.

CHAPTER FIVE

Uncle Albert Gets Better

Mama and Aunt Edith come running
out of the hole in the wall that is the
beetle family's front door.

"Oh my goodness!" Mama cries.

"Albert!" Aunt Edith screams.

"He cut himself on a pair of scissors," Marvin tells them.

Mama acts quickly. "Here, help me carry him into the house," she says. Together, they drag the tissue with Uncle Albert on it, while Uncle Albert moans softly.

"Oh, Albert," Aunt Edith sobs.
"Albert. Speak to me."

"I'm a goner," Uncle Albert says. "I'm
badly cut."

Aunt Edith flings herself over him.
"Oh, my darling. What will I do
without you?"

Marvin looks at his aunt and uncle, and thinks that Elaine and her parents are a lot alike.

"Nonsense!" Mama says. "Albert will be fine. Edith, it's impossible to pull the tissue with both you and Albert on top of it."

Still sobbing, Aunt Edith stands up and helps carry Uncle Albert into the living room.

There, Mama looks at the hole in his shell. Marvin thinks it looks better. There is no yellow goo oozing out.

"James helped us," Marvin says. "He put medicine on the cut."

"Thank heavens for James," Mama says, and Marvin feels a swell of pride that he has such a good friend.

"Well, it stopped bleeding," Mama says. "And it's a small, clean cut. I think it will heal just fine. Are you in pain, Albert?"

"Ahhhhhhh," Uncle Albert moans. "Yes! The pain is terrible."

"All right," Mama says. "I will get you some of the pink pill."

Marvin knows that the pink pill is very special medicine. It makes pain go away. Mr. Pompaday calls them "baby aspirin" and takes them every day for his heart. Sometimes he drops one. This is exactly the kind of thing the beetles like to find when they go collecting . . . though Marvin and Elaine aren't allowed to touch human pills because they are so powerful.

Mama comes back with a tiny bit of the pink pill and feeds it to Uncle Albert.

Just then, Papa and Elaine arrive. They've dragged the blue sack to the cupboard all by themselves.

"Oh, my dear, hurt father!" Elaine cries when she sees Uncle Albert. "How are you?"

But Uncle Albert doesn't answer. The pink pill has made him sleepy, and he's dozing.

"Let's take him to the bedroom," Mama tells Papa. "I think he'll be much better tomorrow."

And so the excitement is over.

The grown-ups leave to take care of Uncle Albert, and Marvin and Elaine are alone in the living room with the blue sack.

"Let's look at what we found," Elaine says.

They open the sack and take out the
things from the day of collecting:

The shiny
silver dime.

The bit of
chewing gum.

The orange tack.

And the strange black thing with
the sharp tip that Marvin
found in James's room.

"I'm sorry I was mean about the dime," Elaine says suddenly.

Marvin looks at her in surprise. "That's okay," he says. "You found it. It's a really good thing."

"Yes," she agrees. "But you found something too." She crawls over to look at the thing Marvin found. "It's interesting," she says.

Marvin studies it. It's so smooth and black and shiny.

All of a sudden, he thinks that maybe James didn't mean to throw it away.

"It might belong to James," he says. "I shouldn't have taken it."

"How do you know?" Elaine asks. "It was on the floor by the wastebasket."

Marvin is quiet for a minute. "It just looks like something James would care about," he says. "I'm going to take it back."

"You are?" Elaine asks. "But then you won't have anything."

"That's okay," Marvin says. "I'll find something good next time."

Elaine is quiet for a minute. "Well," she says, "I guess you can share my dime."

"Really?" Marvin says.

"Yes," Elaine decides. "We can share it."

Marvin smiles at her. "Okay," he says. "Thanks!"

Holding the black thing with two of his legs, he crawls out of the house, through the cupboard, and into the quiet kitchen.

It takes a long time to get to James's room because the black thing is heavy, and Marvin has to crawl with only four legs.

When he gets to James's room, he
sees that James is still reading his book.
Marvin crawls across the blue rug and up
the leg of the desk. It's hard to crawl
up the desk!

He keeps slipping.

And once he
almost falls.

Finally, Marvin makes it over the edge, dragging the black thing with him. He puts it in the middle of the desk. Then he runs toward James.

James looks up from his book.

"Hi, little guy! How's your friend? Is he feeling better?"

James drops his book on the bed and sits up. Marvin runs over to the black thing and taps it with his front legs.

"Hey!" James says. His whole face
breaks into a smile. "My shark tooth!"

So that's it—a shark tooth! Marvin knows about sharks because James likes to watch a television show called *Creatures of the Deep*. It's about fish and animals that live in the ocean. Sharks are the scariest of all.

And this sharp little black thing is the tooth of a shark. Marvin can hardly believe it.

James reaches for the shark tooth. "I thought I lost it," he tells Marvin. "I can't believe you found it! It's from the beach when we were on vacation. I brought it back in my suitcase, but then I must have dropped it."

Marvin beams up at him.

James holds the tiny black shark tooth under his lamp.

"You're the best, little guy," James says.

And Marvin is happy.

He is happy because Uncle Albert is going to be okay.

He is happy because Elaine is going to share the dime.

He is happy because he got to go collecting.

But most of all, he is happy because
he made James happy . . . and there is
nothing nicer than making your best
friend happy.

James is taking Marvin to school! Marvin will finally get to meet James's friends and attend art class with him. But then an accident separates the two, and Marvin gets lost. If Marvin ever wants to see his family again, he must find James. But where is he?

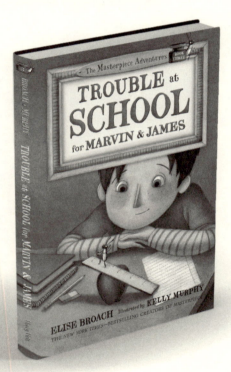

Keep reading for a sneak peek.

CHAPTER ONE

Marvin Goes to School

It's early morning, and Marvin is watching James get ready for school.

"I have Art today," James says. "Mr. Chang is the best. I wish you could meet him."

Marvin has heard James talk about the art teacher before. Mr. Chang tells James, "There are no mistakes, just happy accidents."

This means that if you do something wrong when you're making a picture, it isn't really wrong, because it leads the way to something new.

Marvin tries to remember this when he makes pictures of his own.

For instance, when he's drawing a flower and his leg slips, he can turn the flower into a rabbit, like this:

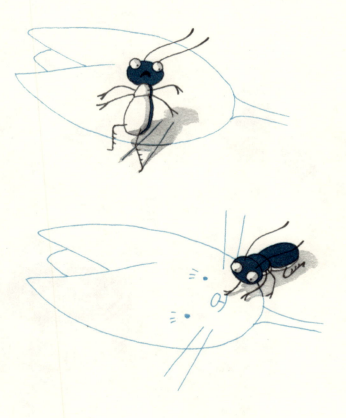

Or when he's drawing a starfish and
he makes too many points, he can turn
it into a dinosaur, like this:

"Hey," James says suddenly. "Why don't you come to school with me?"

Marvin can't believe what he is hearing.

School!

He has always wanted to go to school with James. He's so happy that he runs around in circles.

James laughs. "Does that mean yes? We have to hurry! You can ride in my pocket."

James puts his finger on the desk. For one second, Marvin thinks of Mama and Papa. He knows he should ask them about going to school with James. He thinks they probably wouldn't like it.

But there isn't time. And anyway, he is so excited! He's going to *school*! At school, James has a whole life that Marvin knows nothing about. Now he will get to see James's friends. He will go to Art class. He will hear what Mr. Chang has to say about happy accidents. It will be amazing!

Marvin runs toward James's finger and takes a flying leap.

James lifts him up and drops him gently into his shirt pocket, where Marvin can peek out. Then James grabs his backpack and yells, "Bye, Mom!"

"Good-bye, dear," says Mrs. Pompaday. "Don't forget your lunch." She hands him the brown padded lunch bag that keeps his food cool.

"Ba ba, ya ya!" says William, who is in his high chair, eating breakfast.

And then James swings open the front door of the apartment, and they are on their way to school.

First, they go down the hall.

Then they ride in the elevator.

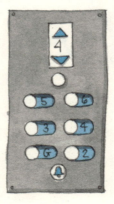

Then they are out on the street.

Marvin loves going outside with James. It's a pretty fall morning. The air is crisp and the leaves are turning red and orange and gold. Marvin is snug inside the warm pocket as he peeks over the top.

The city is full of new sights and sounds. Marvin sees a lady walking five dogs on leashes. He hears the loud, long *honk* of a taxi horn. On a street corner, a man is playing a violin.

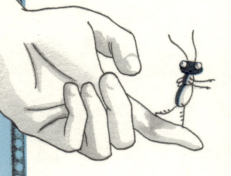

Set off on more grand adventures with Marvin and James!

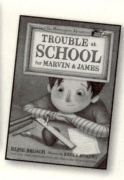